Duck, Duck,

MOOSE!

First Edition • 10 9 8 7 6 5 4 3 2 1 • H106-9333-5-13258 • Printed in Malaysia

Library of Congress Cataloging-in-Publication Data

Bardhan-Quallen, Sudipta.
  Duck, Duck, Moose! / by Sudipta Bardhan-Quallen ; illustrated by Noah Z. Jones.—First edition.
      pages cm
  Summary: Duck and Duck busily prepare for a party, while their housemate, Moose, only gets in the way.
  ISBN 978-1-4231-7110-2—ISBN 1-4231-7110-1
  [1. Roommates—Fiction. 2. Ducks—Fiction. 3. Moose—Fiction. 4. Parties—Fiction. 5. Surprise—Fiction. 6. Humorous stories.] I. Jones, Noah (Noah Z.), illustrator. II. Title.
  PZ7.B25007Duc 2014
  [E]—dc23   2013012211

Book design by Whitney Manger • Reinforced binding • Visit www.disneyhyperionbooks.com

To B (duck), B (duck), and S (moose)—S.B.Q.

For my two favorite troublemakers, Eli and Sylvie—N.Z.J.

Duck, Duck,

MOOSE!

by Sudipta Bardhan-Quallen
pictures by Noah Z. Jones

Disney • Hyperion Books
New York

duck,

duck,

duck,

duck,

duck,

duck,

duck,

duck,

duck,

duck,

 duck,

 duck,

duck,

duck,

moose.

duck,

duck,

duck,

duck,

duck,

duck,

moose?

moose!